SPACE MASH

BY KNIFE & PACKER

Kane Miller
A DIVISION OF EDC PUBLISHING

First American Edition 2016
Kane Miller, A Division of EDC Publishing

Text and illustrations copyright © Knife and Packer 2015
First published by Scholastic Australia, a division of Scholastic Australia Pty Limited in 2015.
This edition published under license from Scholastic Australia Pty Limited.

For information contact:
Kane Miller, A Division of EDC Publishing
P.O. Box 470663
Tulsa, OK 74147-0663
www.kanemiller.com
www.edcpub.com
www.usbornebooksandmore.com

Library of Congress Control Number: 2015938803

Manufactured by Regent Publishing Services, Hong Kong
Printed November 2015 in ShenZhen, Guangdong, China

Paperback ISBN: 978-1-61067-397-6
Hardcover ISBN: 978-1-61067-477-5

MEET THE WHEELNUTS!

Rust Bucket 3000

UPGRADE!
4
ultra-strength magnet

The Rust Bucket 3000 is the most high-tech robot car in the universe. Driven by super-sophisticated robots Nutz and Boltz, this team is always happy to use robo-gadgets to get ahead of the opposition.

The Wheel Deal

Dustin Grinner and Myley Twinkles aren't just car drivers, they are actually super-cheesy pop singers and stars of daytime TV. The Wheel Deal, their super-souped-up stretch limo, is showbiz on wheels!

UPGRADE!
11
singing lessons

Dino-Wagon

This prehistoric car is driven by the Dino-Crew—Turbo Rex and Flappy, a pterodactyl and all-around nervous passenger. Powered by an active volcano, this vehicle has a turbo boost unlike anything seen on Earth!

UPGRADE!
6
super-turbo burn

The Flying Diaper

Babies are great, but they are also gross, and nothing could be more gross than this pair. Gurgle and Burp are a duo of high-speed babies whose gas-powered Flying Diaper can go from zero to gross out in seconds!

UPGRADE!
7
toxic fart

The Supersonic Sparkler

Petrolnella and Dieselina (known as Nelly and Dee-Dee) are fairies with attitude, and with a sprinkling of fairy dust, the Supersonic Sparkler has a surprising turn of speed.

UPGRADE!
11
mega fluff attack

The Jumping Jalopy

This grandfather and grandson team drive a not-always-reliable 1930s Bugazzi. Although determined to win on skill alone, they are not above some "old-school cunning" to keep in the race.

UPGRADE!
8
wheel jack

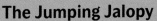

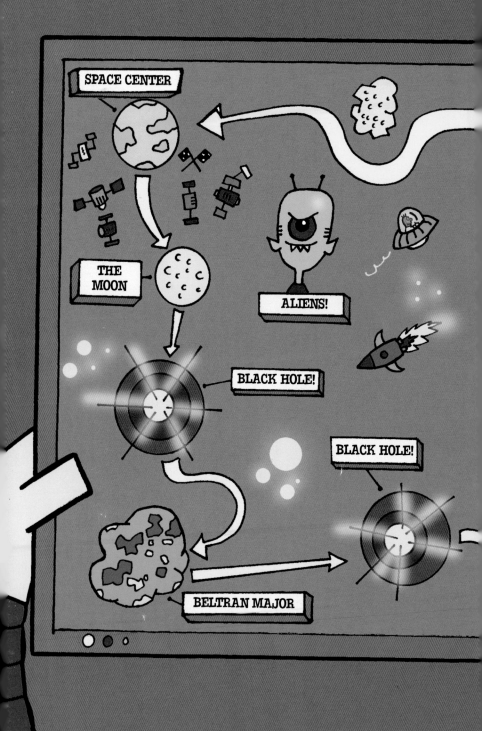

CHAPTER 1

It was the day of the Wheelnuts' third big race—but something important was missing! In a huge fenced-off area in the middle of a swamp were large hangars and rocket launchpads. A safe distance away, an enormous audience waited expectantly—but where were the cars? And where was the racetrack?

Multibillionaire race organizer Warren "Wheelie" Wheelnut had taken the drivers to his specially built Space Center, and he had a surprise in store … like all Wheelnuts' races, this was going to be far from ordinary!

"Howdy and welcome to my Space Center," said the billionaire from the top of a large crane. "Now you may be wonderin' where the cars are? Well, that's simple—there are no cars!" The crowd gasped—a race with no cars! "The third race in the competition is happening in space, and the drivers are startin' the race in … rockets!"

The crowd cheered as one by one the contestants emerged. Their cars had all been customized with rocket boosters!

"The rules are simple—there *are no* rules!" Wheelie continued. "Now let me introduce you to the Wheelnuts themselves!"

Wheelie introduced each team and asked them what they thought of racing in space.

"First up, the Supersonic Sparkler!"

> We're ready to light up the Milky Way and sparkle in space!

"Say hello to the Rust Bucket 3000!"

> Well, for us it's like a "home game!"

"Next we have the Jumping Jalopy!"

> This is one "space race" we have every intention of winning!

"It may be one small step for a dino ..."

"Here's the Dino-Wagon. How do you feel about going into space?"

"but a giant leap for dino-kind!"

"Now, the Wheel Deal!"

"We can't wait to reach for the stars!"

"And finally, the Flying Diaper!"

"We're wearing special "gravity diapers"—so bring it on!"

"So there we have it, ladies and gentlemen. Please give a Space Age round of applause for the Wheelnuts!"

9

"Yes, every car has been turned into a rocket," chuckled Wheelie. "But that's just for the first part of the race—they will then transform back into cars when they reach the moon. There are trophies for the top three drivers and Wheelnut Gold Stars to be won at checkpoints and in the world-famous Wheelnut Challenge," he continued. "Gold Stars can be used at the Wheelnut Garage for car upgrades and cheats!"

It was time for the race to start—but this time there was to be no starting bell or cannon shot. Instead, there was a countdown. Warren's gantry was moved safely to one side and his voice boomed through a megaphone:

"5 ... 4 ... 3 ... 2 ... 1 ... BLAST OFF!!!"

VA-ROOM!

The rockets on the rear of each car simultaneously sparked into action. With a terrific noise, the Wheelnuts zoomed into the sky and the race was underway!

The crowd went wild as the rockets shot up through the clouds. The Wheelnuts may have been used to speeding along roads, but they weren't used to blasting into space, and some drivers were having real problems. But the leading pair was having a great time!

The Flying Diaper was finding the whole experience hilarious.

"This is brilllliant!" said Gurgle.

Second was the Supersonic Sparkler— the wings on their car were folded away and they weren't used to flying *this* high!

"Hold on tight, Nelly! This is fuuuuun!" screeched Dee-Dee.

But if the cars in the lead were enjoying the
experience, the cars at the back were having to get
the hang of heights—and fast!

"I want my mommy!" wailed Turbo Rex.

"I can't look down," sobbed Flappy.

But the course was about to get a lot harder—within seconds of blasting off, the Wheelnuts were out of Earth's atmosphere and zipping through space—and space is full of floating objects, some of them seriously *big!*

"Space junk!" said Campbell. "Tons of it!"

CHAPTER 2

It was now a real test of driving skills and cunning to see who was going to dodge the deadly flying metal, as bits of old satellites and rockets hurtled towards them. But being a Wheelnuts race, it wasn't long before some of the drivers were using the situation to their advantage. And one had a bigger advantage than most—the Rust Bucket 3000. They were used to flying through space and they had the perfect gadget for cheating!

"Deploy robotic arm!" said Nutz as he made some adjustments to the onboard computer.

A huge metallic arm stretched out from the front of their craft.

"Robotic arm deployed!" said Boltz. "Now what?"

"We unleash the brand-new ultra-strength magnet we bought with our Gold Stars!" said Nutz. "What a bargain—enjoy the mayhem!" He pressed a large green button to activate the magnet. Immediately bits of space junk started flying towards it.

CLANG!

THUNK!

"This has a double effect," said Nutz. "Firstly it clears our path, and with a clear path we can go faster."

"Yes, but it's helping the other drivers too," said Boltz. Out of his window he could see the other drivers were now in their slipstream.

"I said a *double* effect, you rust-brained nincompoop!" snapped Nutz. "The SECOND effect is what we *do* with the junk—now, get ready!"

Boltz maneuvered the robotic arm and then Nutz pressed a big red button marked FIRE.

The robotic arm flung the junk straight back into the path of the oncoming Wheelnuts and, just as Nutz had hoped, there was complete chaos!

The Jumping Jalopy took a direct hit from a large chunk of satellite!

Hovering hubcaps!!!

PLING!

The Flying Diaper was showered with metallic debris!

I want to have a nap!

The Supersonic Sparkler did its best to swoop past a lump of old space rocket!

This is really un-sparkly!

PLONG!

PLANG!

The Wheel Deal narrowly dodged a shower of old tin cans!

We don't do heavy metal!

But one vehicle was not going to put up with the metallic bombardment—it was going to fight back!

"Set the volcano to RED HOT!" said Turbo Rex as she dodged the metal missiles.

"Volcano ready!" said Flappy.

"And … BLAST!" said Turbo Rex.

The volcano that was mounted on the rear of the car started to roar, then let out a stream of molten lava.

The sizzling lava melted every piece of metal it hit. The space junk was being vaporized and the Dino-Wagon was now flying past the rest of the competition. In fact, it wasn't long before it was gaining on the Rust Bucket 3000.

"Flappy, crank the heat up to Super-Turbo Burn!" roared Turbo Rex.

Over in the Rust Bucket 3000, things were hotting up.

"Is it me or is it getting warm in here?" asked Nutz. The Dino-Wagon was now so close they could feel the heat.

"My metal underpants are melting!" wailed Boltz. "It's hot, hot, hot!"

As the robots tried to extinguish their underpants, the Dino-Wagon zoomed past them, into the lead!

CHAPTER 3

No sooner had the Dino-Wagon sped into the
lead than it was having to slow down. The next
part of the race was about to start: a moon landing
that was going to require super steering skills and
nerves of steel.

   "Deploy parachute!" shouted Flappy.

Guiding their rockets down onto the surface of the moon was really tricky, but this didn't stop the Wheelnuts from making a race of it. The Jumping Jalopy was descending smoothly when suddenly the Flying Diaper swooped in front of it. Meanwhile, the Supersonic Sparkler went hubcap to hubcap with the Rust Bucket 3000.

One by one the Wheelnuts landed on the moon.
As soon as they hit the dusty surface, their rockets
and parachutes were discarded and their vehicles
were transformed back into cars. The drivers
would have to deal with cavernous craters, choking
dust and zero gravity—this was going to be super
challenging! With a humungous puff of space dust,
the race was back on.

"This is sooo cool!" said James as they bumped
along the track.

"Watch out for that crater!" exclaimed Dee-Dee
as she nudged the Jumping Jalopy towards a gaping
lunar hole.

But one car was nowhere to be seen.

CHAPTER 4

One of the rockets had not stopped on the moon. It had powered straight past it!

But super-cheesy former pop stars Dustin Grinner and Myley Twinkles were merely taking a short diversion. They had set a course for the planet Showtune 7.

"Forget about Gold Stars, our agent has finally found a place that recognizes quality music," said Myley.

"And we are going to give them a performance they will never forget!" said Dustin.

Showtune 7 came into view and, as they had hoped, a huge crowd had gathered—a crowd that LOVED them!

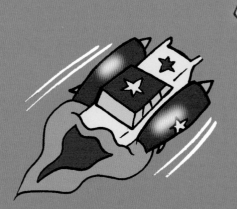

"Please give a great big Showtune 7 welcome to Dustin Grinner and Myley Twinkles!" said the alien MC as the crowd went wild. The pop duo was soon singing all their greatest hits and the crowd of aliens danced and sang along. But then the worst thing that could ever befall a pop double act happened … silence!

"Microphone malfunction!" wailed Myley. "Our fans can't hear us!"

"Even the one with twelve ears," said Dustin, pointing to an alien in the front row.

The crowd was getting restless when a little alien stepped forward. "My name is Laxalon Pi," he said. "I am also a singer, and would be honored if you would use my microphone."

"You're just toooooo cute," gushed Myley as she took the microphone.

"Yeah, high five, alien singing dude!" said Dustin. But before the alien could reply, the duo started to sing with the new microphone. And what happened next was something that even showbiz veterans like Myley and Dustin had never seen before. The microphone was *so* loud that the stage cracked, the stadium windows shattered and the roof blew off! And although the preening popsters loved the sound of their own voices, even *they* had to cover their ears. At first they weren't sure what to do, but when the crowd went wild, they sang even louder!

BOOM!

While Myley and Dustin are singing their final hit, let's take a closer look at their car as we put the Wheel Deal UNDER THE SPOTLIGHT!

Totally Rad Recording Studio: to record that next hit on the road!

Starstruck Spotlight and Pyrotechnics: vital for a fabulous show (and occasionally for driving)!

Glitter-filled Hot Tub: for added sparkle while relaxing!

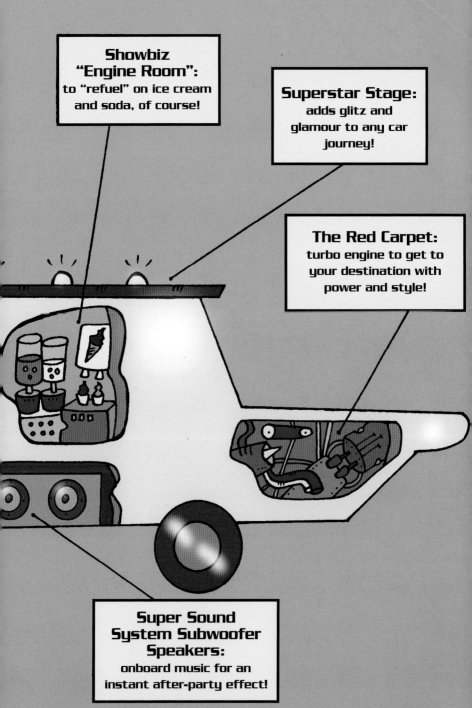

Showbiz
"Engine Room":
to "refuel" on ice cream
and soda, of course!

Superstar Stage:
adds glitz and
glamour to any car
journey!

The Red Carpet:
turbo engine to get to
your destination with
power and style!

Super Sound
System Subwoofer
Speakers:
onboard music for an
instant after-party effect!

As the crowd went totally bonkers and Miley and Dustin prepared to perform yet another encore, they suddenly remembered that they had other business …

"The Wheelnuts race!" said Dustin.

"It's a shame we have to leave these adorable fans behind—but we have a race to win!" said Myley.

With no time to return the borrowed microphone, the cheesy pop duo took a final bow, hopped in the Wheel Deal and blasted off to the moon.

ZEEOW!

SHOWTUNE 7

CHAPTER 5

T he Wheel Deal landed smoothly but had some
ground to make up on the other racers. Myley
put the souped-up limo into overdrive and they
soon had the Wheelnuts in their sights.

At the front of the pack, the challenge was who
could handle the terrain best. That and the zero
gravity—things just kept floating upward! In the
lead was the Jumping Jalopy. Heavy, old-fashioned
sports cars, it seemed, were ideal for moon driving.

But they wouldn't hold the lead for long
because Campbell was struggling—with his
moustache!

"I just can't see the course!" said Campbell. The ends of his moustache were floating up and covering his eyes. "I knew I should have had my moustache trimmed!" he wailed.

James was doing his best to hold down the disobedient facial hair. As they swerved across the course, the other drivers were quick to take advantage.

The Supersonic Sparkler had a completely different approach to the lack of gravity. They weren't fighting against it—in fact, they were *using* it.

"This is perfect," said Dee-Dee. "Our sparkly wings are fantastic! We float up, then sweep down, I love being a fairy!"

But the Supersonic Sparkler's wings were now getting seriously clogged up with space dust. From being at the front they quickly dropped back, all the way to last place—even the Wheel Deal was in front of them!

"We have got to get back to the front," said Dee-Dee as she surveyed the cars ahead increasing their lead. "Time for something *really* nasty!"

"You don't mean …" gulped Nelly nervously.

"Oh yes! I mean it's time for a Mega Fluff Attack," said Dee-Dee, pressing a large yellow button.

As you will know by now, in the Craziest Race on Earth there are no rules, but every so often a team does something so bad, so nasty, that if you're easily offended, you should look away. Because the Supersonic Sparkler was about to unleash its "SUPER-SICK MEGA-NAUGHTY CHEAT."

SUPER-SICK MEGA-NAUGHTY CHEAT!

A large funnel, bought from the Wheelnuts Garage, slowly emerged from their vehicle. When it was in place, Dee-Dee pressed FIRE!

A high-powered blast of pink fairy dust flew into the air. The effect was instant! The magic dust began to form huge fluffy creatures, creatures that targeted every other car on the circuit.

"We're being butted by a giant unicorn!" wailed Nutz in the Rust Bucket 3000.

"A huge purple bunny is nibbling my moustache," said Campbell, who could no longer steer the Jumping Jalopy.

THUNK!

The Dino-Wagon and the Wheel Deal were also at a dead stop as a huge pink fairy tickled them with her wand.

The Flying Diaper was shooting around in a circle, trying to shake off a huge polka-dot pony.

The Supersonic Sparkler simply cruised past them all and into the lead!

"Warren Wheelnut might as well just hand the first-prize trophy to the Supersonic Sparkler right now," said James as he and his grandfather were cornered by the big purple bunny.

The Flying Diaper was not doing any better.

"It looks like this pony is 100% drool proof!" bleated Gurgle as they blasted it with baby dribble.

Fortunately one car did have a solution …

"We must have a gadget in here somewhere," said Nutz as he scanned through the various robotic attachments they kept on board.

They had almost given up when Boltz had a brain wave. "The vacuum attachment!" he said.

Although the Rust Bucket 3000 could have made it a two-car race with the Supersonic Sparkler, they wanted a real race, so within seconds they had vacuumed up *all* the giant fluff monsters.

SHWOOP!

The other Wheelnuts cheered—the race was back on. And everybody wanted to get even with the Supersonic Sparkler!

"We've got to get back at those pesky fairies!" snarled Myley.

"Just wait till I get my claws on them," growled Turbo Rex.

CHAPTER 6

While the Wheelnuts get back on track, let's take a closer look at that big lump of moon rock over there. That's right, the big lump of moon rock that seems to be chuckling.

You'll notice that this is no normal moon rock: a normal moon rock doesn't laugh, a normal moon rock doesn't have hair or a chin. Because *this* moon rock is actually Waylon "Wipeout" Wheelnut in disguise! Wipcout is Wheelie's less successful, more angry brother. His mission in life is to sabotage Wheelie's races—even the ones that take place in space!

"These fools have no idea what I have in store for them," cackled the evil second-rate race organizer. "Is everything in position, Dipstick?"

Wipeout's sneaky sidekick, Dipstick, appeared out of the dust. He had been disguised as a lump of space debris.

"Yes, master—your top scientists have created a really nasty piece of equipment."

"Excellent," said Wipeout. "Now let's move into position so we can get them!"

"Hop on the space buggy," said Dipstick as he uncovered their hidden space vehicle.

"To our space rocket at top speed!" said Wipeout.

"At top speed!" repeated Dipstick. But their spacecraft didn't move. Not an inch.

"What's wrong?" barked Wipeout. "Make it go!"

"Rust, sir, heaps of the stuff," said Dipstick, looking at the motor.

Wipeout reached for his mobile phone and dialed.

"Hello, intergalactic car breakdown service?" said the nasty villain. "I need a tow truck—now!"

CHAPTER 7

As Wipeout waited for a space tow truck, the first checkpoint was in sight—and checkpoints meant gold stars!

In first position was the Supersonic Sparkler— their super-sick cheat had given them a big lead, but gaining on them were some angry Wheelnuts!

"They're catching up!" wailed Dee-Dee. "They seem to have shaken off the fluff monsters …"

"If we can just hang on until the checkpoint," said Nelly as she pushed their car to the limit. Up ahead they could see a giant loop the loop.

As the cars barreled through the loop the loop they went flying into the air. The checkpoint was the entrance to a black hole that was going to shoot them even farther into outer space!

The Supersonic Sparkler was just about to pass through when they heard a loud raspberry noise and a green gas enveloped their cockpit. The Flying Diaper had unleashed a toxic fart and the Sparkler was malfunctioning!

"Hooray for our Gold Star upgrade!" said Burp.

The Flying Diaper squeaked past the Jumping Jalopy, but the Supersonic Sparkler managed to hang on to third place.

RRRRIP!

They were swept up into the black hole and sent spinning through a long narrow tunnel for what seemed like forever. Finally they could make out a light in the distance and one by one they shot out of the vortex and onto the surface of a strange-looking planet. There, standing by his private supersonic intergalactic jet and wearing a protective suit, was Warren "Wheelie" Wheelnut himself!

A rootin' tootin' welcome to deep, deep space, Wheelnuts! Congratulations on some extra-ordinary drivin' ... and cheatin'! Let's look at who earned the most stars!

BLACK HOLE CHECKPOINT

1 Flying Diaper

2 Jumping Jalopy

3 Supersonic Sparkler

4 Rust Bucket 3000

5 Dino-Wagon

6 Wheel Deal

The stars: 6 stars for first place, 5 stars for second place, 4 stars for third place, 3 stars for fourth place, 2 stars for fifth place and 1 star for sixth place.

"And now it's 'Wheelnut Challenge' time!" said Wheelie. "This planet is Beltran Major—which has a really, really bad atmosphere that will make you prickle, tingle and beg for mercy. You will all get a protective suit. The bad news is each suit contains a 'surprise' and the challenge is to see who can keep their suit on the longest. I call this challenge, 'Hey, Dude, There Are Robot Ants in My Space Underpants!'

"When you've had enough, just shout, 'I'm a Wheelnut, get me out of here!'

"Now please go and get changed!"

The Challenge was on! With their leathery skins designed for hot weather, Flappy and Turbo Rex were soon feeling decidedly chilly. Wheelie had filled their suits with ice cubes, eels and a giant squid!

Cold, slimy, and that's just the squid! I'm a Wheelnut, get me out of here!

Itchy, itchy ... I'm a Wheelnut, get me out of here!

The Wheel Deal's suits were designed to make them itch. They soon found their skin covered in sand, cockroaches—and a mouse!

The Flying Diaper's suits were filled with something they should have been familiar with— drool. But this wasn't ordinary drool, this was *toxic* drool and the effect was a bit like having an army of red ants dancing on your skin!

The Rust Bucket 3000 crew was not faring any better. Their suits were filled with a sticky liquid that was melting the metal on their arms and bodies!

Only two sets of drivers remained: the Supersonic Sparkler fairies, whose suits were filled with the least fluffy products you could imagine— all kinds of bristly things including prickly cactuses and spiky twigs …

And the Jumping Jalopy, whose suits were filled with disgusting smells, including rotten eggs and old socks …

Who was going to last the longest? Dee-Dee and Nelly were feeling just about OK until a strange creature started to crawl up to the top of their suits.

Eek! What kind of spiny brute is this? Get off my nose!

Miniature space hedgehogs! I'm a Wheelnut, get me out of here!

The last team standing was the Jumping Jalopy—no matter how yucky and foul-smelling their suits got, James and Campbell were not budging!

If you close your eyes tight, you can get to like the aroma of three-year-old gym clothes ...

The challenge was over and after a quick shower and change of clothes, the drivers were all back with their cars.

"Congratulations to the Jumping Jalopy—they have been given **5 bonus Gold Stars** for winning the Wheelnut Challenge!" declared Wheelie.

"You can use the Gold Stars to buy a moustache trimmer," chuckled James.

CHAPTER 8

"It's time to get back to racing, everyone," said Wheelie. "You are about to discover even more planets … because the next part of the race is all about planet hopping! Follow the course—it will lead you through strange and exciting new worlds … good luck!"

The drivers were back in their cars and on the move. As they set off once again, they approached the entrance to another black hole …

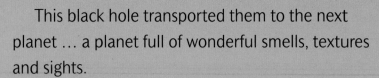

This black hole transported them to the next planet ... a planet full of wonderful smells, textures and sights.

"This course seems delicious," said Campbell.

"Good enough to eat!" chuckled Dee-Dee.

The Wheelnuts had landed on planet NoshNosh, where everything was made out of food!

The first problem was the temptation to stop!

"That river is full of apple puree!" said Gurgle. "Even the clouds are made of chocolate. Let's stop—I'm starving!"

"That tree is a giant chicken leg!" said Turbo Rex. "A quick nibble won't do any harm …"

But as some of the drivers thought about pausing for a pit stop, the rest were shooting ahead. The race was still on!

"No time for snacking!" said Dustin as the Wheel Deal struggled to keep control on a road that was made of bread and jam.

SQUELCH!

The Jumping Jalopy had decided now was
the time to make their move. As the other cars
struggled with the sticky terrain, Campbell used all
his driving skills to put them in first place.

"Great driving, Grandpa!" said James. "I just love
the way you glided over that chocolate bridge and
had the pork chop mountain for breakfast!"

Campbell was certainly enjoying the driving, but a quick look behind told him the rest of the field was catching up.

"They're getting the hang of the course," said Campbell. "I think we need to make the most of our strong start."

"How?" asked James.

"Time for some old school tomfoolery—or as you youngsters call it, 'cheating!'" chuckled Campbell. "And that mountain of meatballs has given me an idea!"

Campbell quickly parked the Jumping Jalopy
behind the large mound of steaming meatballs.

"A little 'slippage' with some help from our
upgrade should ensure we get into the lead," said
Campbell. He stepped out of the car and carefully
placed the wheel jack at the foot of the pile of food.
"Now when I give the signal, heave!"

The rest of the Wheelnuts came skidding around a turn. James and Campbell cranked the wheel jack and the pile of meatballs began to teeter …

"To the next planet!" laughed James as they sped away. Just as Campbell had hoped, the other Wheelnuts were buried in meatballs!

"Sauce overload! Sauce overload!" screeched the Rust Bucket 3000's onboard computer.

"The Sparkler's wings are covered in sauce!" wailed Nelly.

"Meatballs?!" complained Burp. "Not cookies?"

"This is NOT on my diet!" wailed Myley.

But one set of drivers saw this as an opportunity and not a problem. Turbo Rex had crawled out of the Dino-Wagon and reached deep into the volcano to grab a knife and fork.

"One for you and one for me," said Turbo Rex. "Flappy, we're going to eat our way out of this crisis!"

The two dinosaurs were soon gobbling, munching and slavering their way through the food obstacle …

CHAPTER 9

But as the drivers chomped their way back onto the course, what they didn't know was that they were being watched! High in the sky above them hovered a mysterious spaceship—but it wasn't being flown by aliens or robots. It was being flown by Wheelie's evil brother, Wipeout!

"This planet made out of food is giving me an appetite," chuckled the villain.

"I told you to have some lunch before we left," said his sidekick, Dipstick. "I may have an old sandwich in my ..."

"An appetite for EVIL!" barked Wipcout. "I have no time for 'old sandwiches'—now get the laser in position!"

Dipstick flicked a switch and a hatch on the top of their spaceship slowly opened.

"Now to take aim," said Wipeout as he used a joystick to target the laser. "The meteor shower should be passing overhead any moment … NOW!"

Wipeout pressed FIRE and a laser beam shot high into the dark sky above them.

"Now to sit back and enjoy the DEVASTATION!" howled Wipeout.

BLAMMO!

Back on NoshNosh, the race was in full swing, but no one was aware of what was happening high above them. Flappy and Turbo Rex had eaten their way through the entire mountain of meatballs. Despite feeling a bit bloated, they were making good progress catching up with the Jumping Jalopy. At the back of the pack, the Supersonic Sparkler (which had finally gotten all the tomato sauce off its wings) was neck and neck with the Wheel Deal.

But everyone hit the brakes when they heard an enormous BANG in the sky above them!

"I just love this planet," said Gurgle. "Look what's coming out of the sky now—strawberry ice cream!"

"Grab a spoon, guys, this is going to be fun!" said Burp.

"Look at those fools," laughed Wipeout. "They have no idea what's going to hit them. This race will be over in minutes and my brother will be finished!"

CHAPTER 10

The course was not being pelted with ice cream—it was being bombarded by huge chunks of molten space rock!

The cars couldn't take much more. They had to find cover, and fast!

"We need somewhere to hide!" said Dee-Dee.

"Look, there's a gap in that chocolate brownie," said Nelly. "Everyone, follow us!"

The cars all zipped through the gap. They were safe for now—but the huge brownie shook and juddered.

"I don't think this will hold out much longer," said Nutz. "We need to find out what's causing this meteor shower and stop it. Man the periscope!"

A large metal periscope emerged from the top of the Rust Bucket 3000 and poked out above the top of the brownie.

"OK, I can see meteorites falling from the sky," said Boltz.

"Zoom in closer," said Nutz. "The onboard computer informs me that no meteor shower is scheduled in this nebula. Is something sending them our way?"

"Wait! There's a spaceship—with a laser on it," said Boltz. "It's Wipeout! And he's blasting the meteorites down on us!"

"Sounds to me like we are going to have to bring that spaceship down," said Dustin.

Just then a chunk of brownie was smacked by a meteor, splattering chocolate onto Myley's head. "We need a plan, RIGHT THIS MINUTE!!!" she squealed.

Now, although the Wheelnuts were fiercely competitive, if the race itself was under threat then they were more than happy to team up and fend off whatever was threatening them.

"Well, we have a planet made out of food and a rogue spaceship," said Campbell. "I think it's time for a food fight that Wipeout will never forget!"

As falling meteors shook the whole planet, the Wheelnuts came up with a plan ...

On Campbell's signal, the Wheelnuts put their daring plan into action. First of all, he and James quickly identified the hardest foodstuff on the planet: Space Rock Cake.

The Flying Diaper crew used a ground-shattering burp to dislodge some chunks of the cake.

The Supersonic Sparkler crew then used magic dust to transport the chunks over to the Dino-Wagon.

Myley and Dustin sang some super-high notes to break the rock up into tiny pieces then loaded it into the volcano.

With the ammo in position, Nutz made some frantic calculations on the Rust Bucket 3000 computer.

This information was passed to Flappy and Turbo Rex, who carefully took aim.

On Nutz's signal, the Dino-Wagon crew unleashed the volcano and the chunks of rock cake were sent shooting straight up into the sky.

"Cake!?" said Dipstick as he spotted the incoming edible missiles.

"I told you I wasn't hungry," snapped Wipeout, just as the cake crashed into their ship.

Wipeout's laser fizzled and stopped shooting.

"My plan has failed!" wailed Wipeout.

Wipeout's ship plummeted from the sky into a giant bowl of spaghetti Bolognese!

CHAPTER 11

I t was now safe to return to the racetrack and the
drivers were back in their vehicles, all roaring
along! But they were about to discover that they
weren't going to be spending much longer on
NoshNosh. The road was getting narrower—steep
cliffs of raisin bread rose on each side—leading
them to a checkpoint. The Jumping Jalopy
had been in front before the meteor storm and
James and Campbell were determined to get the
Wheelnut Gold Stars. But the other drivers were
gaining on them …

The narrow road now reached its final point—a
ramp made out of a huge éclair! The Dino-Wagon
made a last bid to get there first, with Flappy
throwing a large lump of cake at the Jumping
Jalopy—but Campbell swerved at the last second.
Then the Flying Diaper burped a chunk of chow
in onto the road ahead …

That sent the Wheel Deal into a spin
and the Supersonic Sparker wobbled
and lost its grip.

"Come on, Gramps, you can do it!"
said James as he wiped noodles from his
grandfather's face.

"Hold on, here comes the ramp!" said Campbell,
clinging on for dear life.

But in a last-minute maneuver, the Jumping
Jalopy went from first to last place in the time it
took for the Flying Diaper to throw a large slice of
cold pizza at their wheels!

SWERVE!

There was some final jostling for position as the cars were zapped flying across the ramp. "Not another laser!" said Boltz as their vehicle wobbled but remained in first position.

"It is, but according to our sensors, this one is friendly!" said Nutz.

Sure enough they were being teleported to the next part of the race—on the planet Toxicron. As they landed, checkpoint Gold Stars were allocated …

PLANET TOXICRON CHECKPOINT

1	Rust Bucket 3000	
2	Flying Diaper	
3	Supersonic Sparkler	
4	Dino-Wagon	
5	Wheel Deal	
6	Jumping Jalopy	

The stars: 6 stars for first place, 5 stars for second place, 4 stars for third place, 3 stars for fourth place, 2 stars for place and 1 star for ace.

CHAPTER 12

There was no food on Toxicron—apart from bubbling green gloop and some weird plants. It looked quite ordinary and the drivers thought this was going to be a regular race.

"A bit of gunk and some strange-looking foliage," chuckled Dustin.

"There's nothing scary about this place!" said Dee-Dee. "Let's get racing!

"Crank up the power!" yelled Flappy.

But as the drivers vied for position, they started to feel themselves rise into the sky ...

They discovered that the course was actually taking them along the back of a giant alien! Not only that, the alien was not particularly happy about being used as a racetrack.

"The course is *alive!*" screeched Boltz.

"Just hold on tight," said Turbo Rex. "We're used to leathery backs … it seems harmless enough …"

Dee-Dee managed to get their car off the alien's back and onto the ground just as the creature gave off a huge, galaxy-shuddering SNEEZE, splattering the Wheelnuts in all directions!

"Elfin Sneezing Powder, I thought it might do the trick!" said Dee-Dee.

With the rest of the drivers scattered all over the course, the Supersonic Sparkler surged into the lead.

But Warren "Wheelie" Wheelnut had one more challenge for the drivers, and this would be their toughest yet. They were about to be blasted to a planet made entirely of metal, populated by angry robots!

"Hey, guys—a spotlight!" said Dustin gleefully.

"Hey! Over here!" shouted Myley. "Make sure you get our best side!"

But this was no spotlight, *this* was a transporter beam—a transporter beam that was sending the drivers straight to Metalon 4 and its scary robots!

CHAPTER 13

With a series of loud CLANKS, the drivers were dropped off one by one on Metalon 4, where a metal road traveled across a metal landscape.

"This planet is like nowhere I have seen before," said Campbell as they approached the first turn.

"It's just made of metal," said James as they entered a tunnel.

But one of the Wheelnuts had a distinctly bad feeling about this planet—the team on the Rust Bucket 3000 was getting decidedly jittery.

"This place is bad, *really* bad," said Nutz.

One by one, the Wheelnuts drove through the tunnel into an underground city. They were about to discover that the inhabitants of this metal city were far from friendly.

Not only were there robots all around them, it was clear they were not there to watch a race. Soon robots were closing in on the racers—some wanted to deflate tires, others wanted to eat metal!

"Wheelie has gone too far this time," said Dee-Dee as a small robot tugged on the Supersonic Sparkler's antennae.

"I know he wants to make the races exciting," said Gurgle, "but this is ridiculous!" A large robot was deflating the Flying Diaper's tires!

The Wheelnuts looked doomed—and the race was about to come to a nasty end ...

"Wait a second," said Myley. "I know what will save us—a song!"

The other Wheelnuts groaned and even Dustin thought the timing was bad.

"This isn't Showtune 7, Myley," said Dustin. "I don't think they are going to like us here …"

But Myley wasn't planning on being liked, and as she plugged in the superstrength microphone they had acquired on Showtune 7, Dustin immediately got the idea.

"Time to put those Gold Star upgrade lessons to the test!" cried Miley.

The Wheel Deal team started singing louder than ever before and as they belted out their hit, *Robo Love,* at an ear-piercing level, the planet began to shake and robots started to short-circuit.

The rest of the racers blocked their ears and shot away. The race was back on and the metal road was creating mayhem. The Supersonic Sparkler slid into the lead before the Rust Bucket 3000 used its magnet to give itself a boost. In the distance they heard some metallic applause—the Wheel Deal had finished their song and were rejoining the race.

But as the Dino-Wagon sped to the front, they suddenly realized they were heading for a huge hole in the road!

One by one
the cars tumbled
through the hole.

"I can't look!"
wailed Dee-Dee.

"We're
plummeting down!"
wailed Burp.

But just then
the cars all
automatically
deployed their
emergency
parachutes. They
were floating back
down to Earth and
the competition
was now to see who
could land first to
win the race!

The cars were all jostling with one another to make it to the finish line.

The heaviest cars seemed to have an advantage. The Rust Bucket 3000 was plummeting fast, with the Dino-Wagon right behind it. The Wheel Deal limo was in third place and the rest of the drivers were powerless to do anything about it. Well, not quite *all* the rest of the drivers.

"We need some gas," said Gurgle in the Flying Diaper.

"But there is no gas up here," said Burp

"Not *that* kind of gas," said Gurgle. "Watch this!"

As the drivers celebrated there was suddenly a flashing light in the sky—a UFO was heading straight for them! The Wheelnuts and Wheelie all ducked for cover. The UFO landed and the front of the ship opened. Out came a familiar-looking figure.

"Laxalon Pi!" said Myley.

"We forgot to give you the microphone back," said Dustin. "Although it saved more than the show!"

The little alien took the microphone.

"Hey, let's sing a song before you leave!" said Dustin. They started an earsplitting version of their megahit, *Your Love Is Out of This World* …

"Well that's all for this race, but the fourth race starts soon! Now spend your Gold Stars wisely at the Wheelnut Garage," said Wheelie.

"Just think of all the gadgets and cheats we could buy," said Gurgle.

"Or we could blow all the points on giant teddy bears!" suggested Burp.

"It's your choice. But don't forget to join us for Race 4 in the Craziest Race on Earth!" said Warren.

Here is a sneak peek at the next course …